GENOCIDE RED

BY

DAN ARROW

MegaArrowPress, LLC

Genocide Red

By Dan Arrow

Published By: MegaArrowPess, LLC

www.heartfeltnovels.com

© 2011 Dan Arrow

Layout: Cheryl Perez www.yourepublished.com

Cover Design: Dan Arrow and Sean Alonso.

Cover Photo Credit: Sean Aloso www.1shot-photo.com

Basket pattern for back cover: Sherman Indian Museum: www.shermanindianmuseum.org

DEDICATION

To all Native People of the Earth. When you are lost and can't find your way, look back to where you came from, and do not fear starting over. You will find all the answers at the core of your beginning.

ACKNOWLEDGEMENTS

I thank the Creator of the Universe with this written work. It is a great blessing in my life to finally discover how to put it out there after many long years.

I thank my wife Cindy for tolerating me throughout this entire adventure, as she describes it, and my children for driving me to continue searching for my unknown past. Somewhere along the way I gained a desire to tell them about their Great Grandmother Margarita Valencia and Grandma Susie who carried the Daniels name which is why I'm called Daniel, and as a result, why Danielle has been given the name. Christina and Julia are my extremes, 20 years apart, but to see them together is an amazing thing. Their sisterly bond is strong.

I thank those of you beforehand who stop and take a moment to discover something about yourself in my protagonist. He is riddled with contradiction, and worthy of redemption.

We all have the ability to change, but will we?

INTRODUCTION

This very first attempt at the writing process was quite an event in my life. It occurred about seventeen years ago after a dream in which I wrote some notes. That first event was surreal, but powerful enough to move me to do something rather uncomfortable—write *The X Chapter* you will discover after you finish reading *Genocide Red*.

Another sunrise and again I had information to scratch on a pad I'd placed near my bed, having some Idea that there was more to follow after my first thoughts. They appeared to take a completely different direction, but as I've read those initial notes I can see now how they relate. By the third day, I had completed an entire outline comprised of the visions I saw on day two and three. Again, *The X Chapter* was unclear at this point, so I stuffed it away hoping no one would ever find it.

Why was I thinking these things? To what end? For what purpose? If I attempt to shield the fact that I recognized it was a clear message begging to get out, I would blatantly be lying to you in hopes you would purchase this manuscript without being turned off by the metaphysical aspects of how it came about. The totally analytical mind I used to taut would have denounced the thoughts of any god nudging me in any direction for any spiritual purpose. I don't quite understand the world in that way today and this manuscript has given me, in part, the evidence I need to more clearly understand there is more than just my own mere creative thoughts bouncing around in the limited space between my ears.

I'd always been one to think of my dreams as being of significance, especially the three reoccurring ones that would come around every so many years to haunt my thoughts, since I was about eight years old. I had always questioned what their meaning might be, and somewhere along the way I did enough self-examination on the issue and came up with answers that satisfied my curiosity. This "dream" was different—really different. I was left with about four pages of scribble to decipher.

By the way, I have had a very difficult time placing the label "writer" on my forehead. Until *"Gen-Red"* was imputed into my thoughts, I had long since given up the "literary" me. When I was a young teen I was a book worm, searching for what the world could offer through the eyes of others, but by the time I was sixteen years old I was only focused on getting out of my tough high school alive and working a job to begin my long list of careers.

I am fifty years young, hyperkinetic, and still can't sit for very long without getting the jitters and moving off the couch to discover something else to get into. How in the world was I going take the enormous amount of time it takes to type one hundred thousand words? Even more of a challenge, how to accomplish it with an injured wife and young children at home? Life definitely had become challenging on several different levels.

Well, the answer didn't come easy. *"Just get started and hammer it out."* The word "just" gets under my skin terribly. My wife can tell you so. There is no "just" anything for me. I overthink everything and probably have talked myself in and out of more life experiences than I care to keep track of. Fear of success may have even been one of the things that often stopped me just short of greatness. Anyway, this story plaguing my brain was one of those nagging things that just kept coming to the top of my thoughts, with a vengeance. Apparently, the writing and release of this story is something I am supposed to accomplish in life. No matter how many excuses I make for not being able to concentrate on writing.

Seventeen years later, I have written several other manuscripts on the romance fiction side of things infused with a ton of action. *So...What About Love?, Love Guru:*

Vigilante Style, Love's Longest Letter, and collecting notes for *Genocide Red Part II* and *III.* In a nutshell, I've learned this: book writing is an extremely arduous process and costs more time, effort, and money than one might think. Yes, to produce an ebook is less costly by far, but if you expect to sell a number of books it takes money to market them.

Originally, I sent *Genocide Red* out to many Native American friends since the story is derived from my heritage. One response from the many stands out above the rest: "I cried through it the second time I read it because this is exactly what is happening to our people." She was a concerned leader of her tribe. Another native friend was so moved by a segment of the story, he sent me a Navajo critter flute. I actually learned how to play it.

I've been asked often if Danny and the author (me) are one in the same. I am an assimilated native that caught another bug of researching my genealogy just before the creation of *Genocide Red.* That adventure reached its end after about four years of digging through old log books, micro phish in several archives, and files with sometimes nothing but an envelope without the letter sent from Sherman Indian School to my grandmother. This manuscript reveals the mentalities and thinking that occurred in the lives of the men in my family. Yes, Danny is me, and my dad, and my Uncle Bobby who died from cirrhosis of the liver at only twenty-five years young from prodigal living.

Thank you for taking time out to take this short story in. When it was first scribbled down, I had no knowledge of Greek three act structure, how to write with active speech, or in any particular tense. I moved through the story as the film played in my head, struggling to describe the visions the best way I knew how at the time. This is not to make excuses for why it may appear rough or immature on the literary continuum. I have cleaned it up a bit, but not too much, desiring not to take away from its original raw quality. It's that quality I find most moving when I read or simply engage in conversation with another human being.

My heart to you is that you would strive for more of what life offers in its simplicity after reading this story.

CHAPTER 1

A fight breaks out!

The pit boss, in jacket-n-tie, comes flying from out of nowhere and jumps into the middle of the melee. He wouldn't think of calling for Security you see, *The Card Floor* is his . . . all his. He grabs one combatant by the throat and straight arms the other in the chest. Both card players are swinging at the air frantically . . . cursing profusely.

Danny pops off his chair and throws his cards like a dart in the direction of the dealers face. Disgusted that not one finds its mark, he grabs his few remaining chips and shoves them deep into his empty pockets, clearing his way forcefully past the brawlers. The Pit Boss decides to step aside and let the action continue when his first attempt doesn't quite thwart their desire to get at one another.

Danny looks back at the two who are now making bloody contact with one another's face.

"Security!" Yells the boss. Small specks of blood red can be seen spattering the green card table cloth. These boys are over fifty years old and no one at the other tables could give a rat's behind, they just look up for a second and keep on playin' as if it's all part of the game.

With both palms, Danny slams the push bar on the fire exit doors and escapes to the outside. Finding himself alone, he shields his stinging bloodshot eyes from the brilliance of what seems to be just another dull morning. A light breeze and the fresh air burns his dry throat. He's spent two, maybe three days of self-incarceration in the smoke-filled penitentiary . . . cancer being it's only reward for all the wasted time.

His thousand dollar suit is wrinkled beyond repair from hours of bonding to a high stakes card table stool. The once perfect knot in his Beverly Hills bought tie is but a tiny ball on a noose around his slender neck. Tugging on it during a critical hand of poker gives him away every time. Nervous, greedy sweat from his sticky palm has blackened the silk.

Danny drifts over to a nearby house phone to place a call. He's too tired to stand on his own and finds a piece of railing to prop himself against just outside the casino. Rummaging through his suit jacket pocket close to his heart, past the empty quarter baggie of speed (for medicinal purposes only), he finds his crushed cigarette pack . . . digs out the best of three, and places it between his parched lips. He shoves the pack back in his pocket and is having trouble finding his lighter. *Must have left it at the table.* A passerby seems to understand his struggle and simply hand passes the casinos book of matches into his palm without saying a single word. He strikes one and pauses for a moment to watch it glow, savoring the smell of sulfur. Striking another, he lights up a cancer stick and begins to puff. A thick cloud of uncontrolled smoke blows back in his face. It reminds him of being shackled to the card table, again.

Danny wanders off, thinking about the day his grandmother died. He hears her voice clearly, as if he's ten years old. She used to talk about how life was on the reservation and how he should be concerned about the difficulties that face our generation. He didn't understand then, and still doesn't seem to get it. She lays buried in her full sized bed on sheets she's had for years. Grandpa's been dead for some time now, but you can smell the familiar scent of old flesh in the room. In a weak and groggy voice she prophesies, "They keep trying to shove business ideas down our throats. We know little about such things, and much about life. Our ways will change considerably if you allow such thoughts to infect your young minds."

Danny snaps out of it, viewing his limousine turn the corner for the hundredth time. He thinks hard and wonders if he's become the "They" that Grandma was talking about. As the limo comes to a stop, he's crushing a half smoked cigarette beneath his expensive leather sole. Squeezing the handle, he lets himself in. James remains in the driver's seat because Danny can't stand being pampered, unless of course he barks out orders demanding it. He thinks of his driver as more of a friend, confidant . . . someone to unload his deepest secrets.

James pulls away from the casino, towards the reservation on a twig like road filled with freshly planted vegetation on either side. Unnatural small trees and shrubs have been captured to add a little color to this barren reservation land. The sleek stretch appears out of place too as it speeds down the asphalt where only a dirt road once existed. On both sides, trailers and rock houses have been abandoned for years now. The path winds around a rocky landscape and begins to severely incline as they approach Danny's house, way up on the hill. It reminds him of a mausoleum for the dead as he looks up. It'll be a while before they get through the entry gate and traversed to the peak. Gray cobblestones beneath the limousine tires sound like native drums out of control. Five minutes to the top of the hill.

Danny's life is out of control. No steady rhythm, just chaos and disorder his only rules.

CHAPTER 2

The limo, hot from the climb, anticipates the approach to level ground. James drives by the grand entry to the residence with no less than 33 rooms. Its three tier fountain is perfectly centered spewing sparkling clear water from a magnificent bronze cast dolphin with a sea foam green finish, the only sign of peace and serenity that can be found. Three automobiles, right out of an old gangster movie sit in a half circle around the bronze center piece. The tires haven't been on other than reservation land since *Bugsy* had them towed home.

Danny never enters through the front doors, he just likes to drive by its movie set appeal and leave the picture perfect scene undisturbed.

James swings around to the back of the property and stops near a small wrought iron gate. Danny gets out and swings it open with ease, there is no lock. James continues to make his way around to the garage. Danny begins to stroll up a path with dense vegetation above and on both sides, his jungle . . . his Eden. A narrow concrete path has been poured to make the journey as effortless as possible. Very little light breaks through the lush green foliage, which has been cut so that only one person, single file, can make it through at a time. Even a drunk could find his way home.

Fragments of growing up seep into his mind as he walks the skinny path. When he was small he didn't understand poor. What is poor anyway? Native Dancing, Bird Singing, Grandfather old but still able to grasp him firmly by the hand and pound out a rhythm like thunder below his feet. A full rich life of fond memories. Poor sounds really good right now. *A step up from destitute.*

Danny enters a clearing where the grass is at attention. Not one blade is out of formation. To the left is his workshop where all the latest tools for making just about anything can be discovered. No time for trivial things. He seldom has time to create anything except havoc anymore. Turning towards the green house on the right, attached to the back of the mansion, he steps through the glass door of the hothouse into a thick sticky mist, like the days before man knew rain. Moving swiftly passed all types of flowers, roots, and vegetables under arrest here, his only focus is to get through the screen door and into his sanctuary.

Taking his shoes off in the entry, he desperately plops his feet firmly on the hallway floor, and lets out a sigh of relief as the slats feel like ice on his swollen toes. Straining to determine which direction to take down the long corridors, he makes his head hurt at having to think. Large sliding glass doors are wide open with long white curtains wildly dancing on a breeze. He can't make a move without delicate mesh material brushing the back of his un-calloused hands.

Bird Singing plays inside his head . . . an annoyance at best. He takes a left, and parallels a wall cluttered with numerous photographs. After walking for about twenty seconds, he stops halfway down the hallway and turns to face a particular set of images. A path is worn in the carpet where he worships the memories as if they were religious statuary. The children are dressed well and enlisted in the finest schools money can buy. His eyes are fixed on the most beautiful woman, then turns away remorsefully. He continues on down the hallway . . . the family was his.

This building, this place in which he's caged, is like a warehouse after hours just waiting to be useful. There's only one occupant these days and even he is empty. Void within.

CHAPTER 3

8 AM.

Extremely fatigued, Danny drags himself into the living room after having stumbled several hundred feet through a myriad of doorways. He stammers over to the entertainment system that covers the entire wall, and jams a CD into the tray to soothe his irritation . . . heading for the stairs to search for something resembling rest. The sweet sound of native flute pierces the air and soothes his throbbing brain. *His heritage has been reduced to but a circular plastic disc.*

Leaping onto the first step, deteriorating by the time he hits the sixth, and then stopping to catch his breath on the seventh, with many more to go. *"Where has my life gone?"* Up eight more and he hits the wall of exhaustion. Hair is sticking straight out on the back of his neck as a result of a perceived presence in the room he just stepped out of. Shadows sway enthusiastically to the sound of a large deep drum and begin to stir his inter most being. A flame that has turned into just an ember. Danny turns to look over his shoulder and see if a dance is really taking place below, but turns away quickly in disbelief convincing himself to shrug it off as a tired man's blurred vision. He stands still for a moment trying to breathe deep and steady his breath. Maybe it's the alcohol from the now empty flask he drags around with him like a baby's bottle that's taken his life away. Darting on adrenaline, he manages to make it up the rest of the stairwell and pauses at the top. Again, having to labor choosing something as simple as his left or right . . . a chore to think.

Danny turns right this time and walks directly into a dead end . . . the closet. The smallest room in the house at 15 X 25 feet. A reminder of Cynthia and the peaceful life they lived before the big business opportunity came along. Their tiny little cracker box trailer was about the same size as this closet where a multitude of the finest suits now hang. A vision of her, seated at their heavily painted wooden kitchen table, captivates his mind. She grinds out the best homemade tortillas while belting out a song her grandmother used to sing in what's left of their native tongue . . . filling in the blanks with hums and hahs. Turning towards him with a warming smile. Danny extends his hand as she places her corn meal covered fingers into his earthy palm.

The pleasant thought is perverted by another more recent account. Cynthia screaming at the top of her lungs, "You don't love me as much as you love your money and card playing! The children don't even know you anymore!" Distraught, in tears, throwing things and self about the room . . . whaling a wretched screech. *Pigs being slaughtered.*

Danny rushes out of the closet, slamming the door behind him, leaning back heavily against it. Unaware why he even stepped in, he bolts toward the double doors at the end of the hallway trying to run away from his past.

Sweat is forming in his hairline when he reaches the end and grabs two large brass handles with both hands, pauses for a moment to notice his stench – guava? Then, jerks on the icy metal handles to unveil a room with an elaborate white marble floor and two large matching gold sinks. The walls are covered entirely with glistening mirror tile. The toilet looks more like an ornate alabaster alter instead of a place for waste. That's a thought! Dropping his pants, he takes a seat and places his elbows on the tops of his thighs. He cups his chin with his palms, as if waiting for another false prophet to dispense a miracle. Danny stares at himself in what seems like a carnival's house of mirrors and decides there's nothing funny about what he sees gazing back. Unshaven, hair is out of place, feeling as baggie as the skin under his red veined eyes. He grinds his teeth at what he sees and snarls, "What are you?" Danny stands to peel his clothes off and bends to untie his shoes, but he has to fight through his pants around his ankles covering them up. Everything is a fight. Literally, everything hurts today. He discovers one lace has already come loose through the course of the day without his approval. *"One less thing to bother with."* He reaches into the shower turning on the water, nice and hot. Stepping out of his suit, as a snake shedding skin, he stares at his smelly pile for a moment. Picking it up, he brings it to his nose and takes a whiff, "Eeew." Danny tosses the wad into the corner of the restroom as if it were mere trash . . . only another thousand dollars down the drain. *Chump change.* The water's blazing hot and Danny's image is fading in the mirror as he watches it disappear into the steam filled room. He turns the cold water on to make it as lukewarm as his heart, steps into the shower and thinks to remember his tie for a split second. Laughing hysterically, he's not able to remember where it got away.

Standing listless with his head tilted back and eyes closed, he reaches to turn the water up again to blistering hot and feel just what Hell might be like. Flaming beads of water spill over his aching frame and feels way too good for human consumption. Standing almost comatose, his labored breathing echoes to the core of the earth where the *Devil* makes his home.

CHAPTER 4

A native brave in the middle of a tropical rain with breastplate and spear, face painted for war—half red, half white. Looking up into the heavens as fire droplets burst across his face. Suddenly, the weight of a drenched business suit, leather shoes soaked through to his silk stockings, a warm fluid fills them to the brim. He stands in a blood red puddle and feels like a Mafioso who's earned himself a pair of cement shoes.

Still in the shower, Danny convulses as if a spear has pierced his rib cage. A sharp slicing pain sends him into warrior mode again, ready for a fight, and finally back to naked man from where he began. He's been driven to his knees.

Danny slithers out of the shower and doesn't bother with something as simple as a towel, then slides into a darkened room, watching his back as if being stalked.

Slamming the door behind him as loud as he can. "If a door slams in the forest, and no one's around to hear it . . . never mind." No windows to allow any light to creep in, only the crack under the door. He topples face first into the cushion of some old piece of familiar furniture. The cover, a cool musty sheet, is soothing against the roughness of his cheek. Eyes like lead almost shut, he hasn't any care . . . any direction. This is where his tormenting begins . . . more nightmares to cloud any chance at a clear unpervert thought.

***

Danny's fog lifts and he's been strapped to a royal looking chair from some mid-evil era. Maybe it's just a piece of left over 70's junk. From head to toe, he looks like the victim of some sick joke. Wrists, chest, and ankles are bound to the gold riveted black leather material. The dry taste of cotton irritates the back of his throat. His gag has been stuffed too deep with no intention to ever retrieve it, and a red plastic toy ball is kept in place with several more straps attached to his bridal. He's held hostage, waiting to become victim to some kind of detestable sort of flick. *A horse gets better treatment!*

Danny is seated at the head of a large elongated conference table that seats seven. Some native, some not . . . one is female. All are dressed in standard business attire and fixed to their puffy high-back leather executive chairs, with intense anxiety in the air. Danny feels awkward and underdressed in his pure white satin PJ's. No slippers to cover his ice cold feet. The group lines both sides of a solid oak boardroom table. The members are brainstorming about something big, but the language is garbled and deceptive, like demons. The group seems to agree on something and the woman at the far end of the table reaches behind her back to select an item from the wall rack. Just as a pool pro would examine her cue, she pulls a dull spear off the wall and checks it out before lining up on the target. She rears back with a beautiful over the shoulder throw. All Danny sees is the tip of the spear for an instant, feeling the burning of something foreign embedded into the flesh and muscles of his abdomen. There's a second of complete silent, something surreal like shock, then his blood spews up and over the edge of the table. The others continue the debate and pause again, allowing the archer to place another blow a little higher and center mass. It blasts Danny's upper chest and spurts a large red glob directly into the face of a native family member seated to his left, unmoved by the warmth of his brother's blood. This time, the non-native businessman to the right squints at the horror and has to turn away. Red streams flow off Danny's seat and onto a piece of clear plastic that was under his chair to protect the expensive plush carpet. The language at the table becomes clear and the idea of a casino business is tossed into the pit. The vicious one pulls a tomahawk from under the table and wields it high.

The Blades edge inches in slow motion towards Danny . . . then the handle . . . the blade . . . faster, handle, blade, faster, handle, and blade. A loud crack is heard, as if a watermelon has fallen from a truck. All cheer as the winning point has been scored in their favor. Danny's vision is blurred by the blood oozing down into his eyes. He can only see what he thinks is his nose in front of his . . . . no, wait! It's just an ax handle.

This game's been won . . . for now.

CHAPTER 5

Danny shoots straight up out of bed and twists directly onto the ice cold wooden slats. Knees and palms hit the floor first, shaking the entire mansion with a loud beep thud. In a blistering sweat, he reaches up for anything familiar to grasp. Groping for the door he almost pulls the knob off in an attempt to escape the room quickly. With both hands placed on each side of his swollen head, he's playing helicopter in the hallway. Pausing for a moment, he realizes it was just another one of the many nightmares infecting his sleep. Staggering towards the stairwell, hanging onto the rail, his feet move faster than his body is willing to go. He darts through hallways, passed other fright filled rooms, until he makes his way to safety. With his eyes half shut, he drags himself through the doorway, as he does religiously to calm his nerves three or four times a night. He goes straight for the liquor cabinet behind a full-service bar. Spouts are atop whiskey and bourbon bottles that have become bone dry like the dessert he lives in. Lipstick stained glasses are strewn all over the counter from last night's party, or the night before. Some chairs are turned upside down on top of a few cocktail tables, as if someone made an attempt to clean up. As usual, whoever came by just used the place and left it in shambles.

Danny doesn't care as long as his bottle of tequila hasn't been disturbed. Cracking a fresh seal, he tosses the top over his shoulder onto the dance floor, and listens as it bounces off things. It won't be needed ever again. He tilts the bottle to meet his waiting lips. Sweet to the taste, not an intrusion. It's five in the morning, as he rears his head back and catches a glimpse of the clock behind the bar. A big swallow and he slams the half empty bottle of Especial down on the counter. Danny picks up the house phone connected to James' small bungalow, between the tennis court and Olympic size swimming pool, "Pick me up in ten!"

James is hovering in REM sleep, but rises from the dead and navigates toward the restroom to drain his bladder. Afterward, he strains to bend under the sink into the cabinet looking for mouthwash, but find something else instead. Struggling to read the label, he discovers another bottle of Danny's favorite poison. He twists the top off and pops the bottle into his mouth, swishing the contents around like some generic form of wash. "How can he stand to live like this? This stuff is everywhere! In the limo, behind plants in the greenhouse . . . I can't seem to get away from it!" Although he knows the answer. The maid has been instructed to keep it stocked up in every nook and cranny without question. Danny actually plays a game with her to see if she can discover a new hiding place. She gets a hundred dollar bill if she can come up with a new one. *Too much time on his hands.*

James continues pondering out loud, while splashing water on his face to wake up. "This knucklehead pays me $80,000 a year to drive in circles listening to his stories. Sometimes for the third time. I've been stuck here for six years." He pauses to look up and view himself in the mirror. "life is at a standstill, but the money's too good to leave." Gripping both sides of the sink, he takes a deeper look into the mirror. "Thank God I'm not him . . . all that money and no life . . . I'd probably shoot myself dead. Then again, we're the same aren't we? Maybe not? I can leave when I've had enough. He can never separate himself from all this stuff . . . this is his home."

James pulls a fresh suit out of the closet and jumps into it like Robin (diddle daddle diddle daddle diddle daddle dee) and heads for the door while licking his fingers to paste his hair down, adjusts his hair into a ponytail, then kicks the door open, Whamo! Leading to the garage, where the Bat Limo awaits. James reaches into the vehicle and hits a button on the visor to open the retracting aluminum door, jumps into his molded spot on the leather seat, ignites the ignition and pulls out slowly. Then, punches the gas pedal in order to get around to the mansion in time to scoop up *Batman*.

CHAPTER 6

Danny has just walked by a clearing between the house and the jungle, his Eden. Meanwhile, with the motor running, James waits in front of the the little gate for Danny to emerge from the foliage. The moonlight is barely able to make its way through the dense vegetation but illuminates the path beneath his feet enough to get through. Slowing his pace from a fast walk to a melancholy stroll, he begins to daydream of a time when something as simple as his hair was important to him. He thinks back to when he was required to cut his ponytail off in the name of Native Business America. As the speaker for the tribe, they agree he should blend with other politicians, not to be labeled as *lone brave ponytail*. The Chief has hand picked him to represent the tribe, not because of his mild education, but specifically for his ability to speak . . .

representing himself and his people as confident in their quest for position and power in the modern world.

***

Danny drives his dead father's Chevy pickup to a little barbershop that's been there since the town was built. It has always been a place that he's noticed since he was a small child, but was told he was forbidden to enter. Standing outside the door for a moment, he thinks about the task he's been handed. The Chief believes it's best for the tribe to move forward and become part of modern-day politics if they're going to have a chance at surviving the ruthless business they've undertaken.

Breaking through the threshold of the door, Danny stands still surveying the surroundings. No one here today except for a little old wrinkled Mexican man seated in one of only two barber's chairs in the entire place. Legs crossed, black plastic framed glasses, a white smock looking like a doctor, maybe a butcher, intensely focused on the daily newspaper he has clenched in his hands.

Marveling at how the man could not have heard the jingle of the large sleigh bells attached to the back of the front door, Danny wonders if he's deft. They remind him of Rain Dancing, but here they have no rhythm or true purpose . . . just a doorbell. Methodically, the seated man begins to close the paper and climb out of the chair where he's perched. Turning away from Danny, he places the newspaper in the other chair for later. Danny feels like he's interrupting the old one's peaceful moment and is about to take the opportunity to run. With his back still turned, the barber faces a large mirror and still hasn't acknowledged Danny's existence. Before Danny can bolt out the door the man speaks out in a deep firm tone, "May I help you young man?" Gesturing with an open palm for Danny to take a seat.

Danny is silent . . . defiant . . . unable to move his feet. Unbeknownst to him, the barber peers past Danny's shoulder into another mirror and catches a glimpse of the long tightly braided snake he is about to trap. Now he's more persistent about Danny's frozen position on the tile floor and commands, "Sit down boy! It won't hurt." Like a hunter tracking his prey, he whips the cloth collar around Danny's neck like a noose and snaps it tightly from behind. The jackal wastes no time in severing the artery, not hesitating for a moment to even think of sharpening a pair of pointed barber's scissors. They bite into years of culture . . . and in seconds have served their only purpose. The barber tosses the snake like cord into the sink behind him . . . leaving it to suffer and die.

Immobilized from the shock, Danny is expressionless throughout the entire ordeal, feeling as if having been placed in an electric chair. The *sculptor* now chips away with a pair of shears to invade untouched regions. The barber flips the chair around to unveil his new creation.

Looking into the mirror, Danny becomes noxious as he feels his insides coming apart at the seams. Acid is bubbling up in the back of his throat.

Joe, the barber, is unmoved by the acidic stench and keeps to his objective. "Can I have the pony tail to hang above my door as a good luck charm?" Danny's blood begins to boil. Enraged at the callousness of the question, he jumps from his seat. Tearing the now puke soiled cloth from his neck and reclaiming his ponytail from the depths of the sink, he throws a ten dollar bill on top of the newspaper in the second chair before storming out of the shop, slamming the door and knocking the bells off their nail . . . scalped and degraded. Seemingly unmoved, the barber throws the ruined cloak in the trash and begins to clean up all the mess so he can get back to reading the daily news. Business as usual.

CHAPTER 7

Danny finally makes it out to the little gate. James is perched up front with a hot engine and the air conditioning up high waiting for some direction. Danny steps in with a fresh suit and no tie. James knows this means he'll be driving a distance, sightseeing and listening to useless chatter . . . wasting precious time. James makes small talk, "Couldn't sleep again?" Danny just looks up with a smirk and makes eye contact in the rearview mirror. James can only make out a silhouette and the haunting pale blue neon from the limousine's bar reflecting off of Danny's glazed over eyes. James guesses the strongest possibility, "Casino?" Which is the usual response. "I would rather take a walk in the woods to think." *Unusual behavior? The boss is always trying to numb himself from his thoughts, why would he want to go anywhere to think. Maybe he's gonna wander off and finally kill himself?* Not much for conversation, Danny reaches above his head for the divider switch and closes the opening between the two. Placing a hand over his face and propping himself up on the armrest with his elbow, he adjusts into his familiar print in the soft leather seat.

An hour later, James lowers the divider to gently allow the early morning light to find its way back to Danny's face. He isn't moved by it. The limousine hasn't been on the road for almost thirty minutes, but James knows that Danny's too mentally numb to notice. Danny, nor James wear watches. Time doesn't seem to matter. Besides, who cares what time it is when you really don't have anywhere to be? Danny could use the sleep anyhow.

James pours his second cup of pure black coffee, while keeping himself amused with a morning paper he picked up before driving into the mountains. Boss didn't have a clue. James tosses the paper over to the passenger seat and plucks the coffee mug off the dashboard before exiting the limo. Walking around to Danny's door, he gently pops it open. Danny is sprawled out with his head straight back and his mouth wide open, drool seeping out of his mouth and down the side of his throat . . . like a murder victim. James interrupts, saving him from another horrific nightmare, "Time for a walk Boss!" and wraps Danny's hand around a lukewarm cup of Java poured from a thermos. Danny is shaken from his comatose state and takes a big swig of coffee. His taste buds kick in, or in this case kick him back. *Not tequila?* He spits up all over James' shoes. James is unsuccessful at holding back his laughter. Danny, falling for this wake up trick time and time again.

Tossing the rest of the coffee on the ground, Danny slaps the cup back into James' hand, with a grimace. Stumbling out of the limousine like a mole, he throws his hands up to shield his eyes from the brilliant beauty of the forest. "Where'd I leave my shades?"

As his expensive leather shoes find the moist earth, his stance is as unstable as his life. He's stepped into a large glob of mud and looks at James is if it's all another calculated joke. James shrugs and lifts his eyebrows to say he didn't do it. Wandering over to the nearest tree to relieve himself, he takes a second to look straight up at the magnificence of its height . . . he can't begin to see the top from where he's standing. Danny steps to the side, actually thinking about not violating Mother Nature's masterpiece before letting out a sigh and watering the surrounding pine needles. Inhaling, he discovers the fresh vibrant morning air. "Zip!" The stench of his own urine to bring him back to reality. Disgusting. Stepping several feet away, he bends to tie his shoes. They were never tied to begin with. Never mind, he slips one off and rears back like a football quarterback to drill it as far as he can. First one goes long before bouncing off the trunk of a hundred year old pine. He reaches for the other one, but doesn't want to make the effort and just steps out of it, leaving it cemented in the mud. Too much work to pull it out. Discarding his current frustration for a moment, he moves anxiously toward the density of the forest. Unknown territory. Still focused on Danny, James yells out, "Are you gonna be okay?" Danny doesn't answer or even turn his head before disappearing into the tree line.

***

Venturing deeper into the forest, Danny speeds up from a fast walk to a jog. He strips his jacket off with a vengeance and slings it to the ground at his side. Jogs for a minute before doing the same with his shirt. His thin designer dress socks have already worn completely through . . . his bare feet being absorbed by the earth. He begins to run, playing dodge with the trunks of mammoth trees and pine branches from seedlings that have grown the size of Christmas trees. Whipping his arms, stomach . . . one slapping him high on the cheek. He welcomes the slicing pain, as the sap fuses itself to his lifeless skin. His sporadic breathing levels to stable . . . rhythmic, as native drums begin to chase his every step. Faster he runs, faster the beat . . . loader the intensity . . . moving him along on a cloud of desperation.

CHAPTER 8

His warrior self takes shape with blood red dye on one side of his face, bone white matching his breastplate, on the other. Birds, systematically move out of his way, anticipating his direction. They bellow boisterous chirping cries . . . a welcoming committee blowing their trumpets upon a triumphant entry. Two feathers affixed to his braided hair matching the bird buglers feathered dress.

Slowing for a moment, he is returned to his now mud and sweat soiled dress pants, crotch ripped wide open, and one hem undone. He picks up a five foot long thin branch and returns to his former pace, back to native brave. The staff is held well-balanced at his side like an athlete preparing to lunge over a poll. It becomes a spear in his hand. An instrument for gathering food, or providing protection? A clearing can be seen up ahead . . . rays of light bursting through the lush canopy.

Danny makes it into a clearing and flings the spear and self to the ground, arms wide open, hands pointing skyward. He slides several feet before coming to an abrupt halt. His knees used as brakes. Looking up, arching his back, he finds an opening in the midst of skyscraper trees. Rivers of clear fluid are flowing from his war torn eyes. Screaming, "Why have you brought me here?" Every living creature in the forest is aware of his presence.

Danny has every physical thing anyone could ever want, yet no knowledge peace. Placing his hands over his face, he dams up reservoirs of free flowing water coming from the pain he's feeling from his insides. Still on bent knees, he bends over into a ball and rocks back and forth like a child trying to comfort itself.

***

Back at the limousine, James is reading the morning paper propped up on the steering wheel. The large black print reads, **"Government Proposes Reclaiming of Indian Lands."** James peers over the top of the newspaper to see Danny emerged from his forest baptism only wearing a pair of tattered pants. Lashes have appeared all over his skin and what appears to be a walking stick in his hand. James hops out and comes around to open the door as an excuse to question. He quizzically looks Danny over from head to toe. "What happened to you?" Danny really smiles for the first time in what seems like years and places his staff on the floorboard before getting in with some sense of renewed confidence. James closes the door gingerly with a look as if not to disturb the psycho within. Shaking his head in disgust, out of Danny's site, James lightly steps back into the driver's compartment, cautiously driving out of the woods making sure the divider is up and secure for the journey back to the nuthouse. *The state medical facility should be the next stop, but who will right my check?* The tires pick up a cloud of dust as James accelerates to make an escape from whatever demons were in that place.

***

Half hour into the trip, James drops the divider and asks Danny if he's seen the headlines. "I don't have time for that trash. Besides, that's what I pay you for! Fill me in!" "Well boss, this article tries to justify how the government can kick Indians off of government lands . . . since they're wealthy enough to support themselves." Danny's anger rises, "That's enough! Not all of us are rich Indians!"

It's always been the lack of trust planted in the back of Danny's head that the government could do such a thing— anything they want, really. Although, he never was one of those conspiracy theorist types like some of his friends growing up. They'd exercise their freedom of speech and say all kinds of derogatory things about the government any chance they got. And to say it front of a microphone during some kind of a rally . . . sweet. Some of them would have been on the other side of any government, regardless of its ideals. Wearing shirts with former American dead President's with catch phrases like "Your Heroes My Enemies." Pretty bold, but what do you expect from a conquered people who now have a voice?

Danny on the other hand was in the middle, too busy just trying to figure out his own circumstance to jump on any cause.

Marriage was the biggest commitment he'd ever crossed paths with. Even then, he didn't do a very good job of it when he had the chance. True, he loved his Cynthia with everything he had, but sometimes your everything is too small to offer a person with a much bigger heart than yours.

CHAPTER 9

In his workshop, Danny picks out just the right tool and begins to peal the bark away from the branch he's carried out of the woods. Daydreaming, he looks in the large mirror attached to the wall behind the bench and begins to deeply question, *"What was the implication, or many implications, of the article James pointed out?"* He sees himself for a moment as a warrior spirit from over a century past, *"To war, or not to war?"* Realizing where he is in time and place, *"Over what?"* And laughs outwardly at his stupid thought. "Just another twisted bunch of political junk!"

"My people lived a relatively peaceful hunter gatherer existence, little need for war. So why do I feel like putting on war paint and parading around with an overprotective point of view." For the first time in years, he thinks a deeper thought. *"The true enemy may not be outside of ourselve's this time. Most of us went willingly to the slaughter with promises of wealth and power. Now, we fight internal issues of greed and lack of self-control. A great many of us have fallen. Now, all the vultures have to do is sit back and watch us tear each other apart before stepping in to devour the leftovers . . . mission genocide complete!"*

Danny affixes a sharp rock to the staff he found in the forest. An actual spear is emerging from his labor. He's worked on it and contemplated about his life for a whole hour, until the final touch. Whipping out a thin piece of leather from a draw nearest his leg, he uses it to connect his long forgotten ponytail to his current creation.

He enthusiastically moves from the workshop up to the main house feeling he's accomplished something. While moving through the greenhouse, he can actually smell a fragrance today. Not the usual tobacco smell from having spent days in the casino. Left down the corridor . . . right into the living room. Not such a chore today. He reaches the mantle and clears it with a sweep of his hand, spilling everything onto the solid wooden floor, and placing the spear on its new resting place. He wanders upstairs whistling National Emblem, a song he learned while a bugler in a United States Army band. For a moment he thinks about his grandmother and all the stories she told him of the Indian School she went to when she was a little girl. About the boys in their band getting haircuts and being placed in uniforms. It's a century later and he lived it all over again . . . by choice. Danny marches upstairs deflated at his connection to having repeated the past. *This is going to be a long shower.*

CHAPTER 10

Danny is seated in his recliner wearing a solid black terrycloth robe. There's a little cherry wood table to his left and a cigar burning in an old sixties amber glass ashtray. Reaching to pick up the stogie, he watches it burn between his fingers for what seems like years. Lifting it out of old ashes and watching the smoke fill the room, reminds him of smoke signals he can't begin to read. About to place it on his lips, but thinks for another minute before catching a whiff of the rotten smell of burning flesh. Cautiously, he places it back in the tray.

Danny lifts a small photograph without a frame, and moves it into view. Through the rising smoke, he sees a familiar native woman, two little children, and someone resembling himself with something like joy on his face. Placing the photo on the center of his chest, he feels his water table begin to rise. Pulling the photo away from his aching heart, he takes a second glance. Through blurred vision, picture still in hand, he listlessly drapes his arm over the armrest. Lifeless and feeling ancient. His hand naturally opens and the memory floats to the carpet like a feather having lost its bird.

Danny lunges towards the table where his gun has been patiently waiting. Frantically, he grabs the handle and shoves the muzzle deep into the back of his throat, enough to gag. With his finger on the trigger he jerks back on it wildly. The hammer drops with a loud snap. There isn't any bullet, just himself . . . the gun . . . and his heart beating in his finger tip.

He lethargically pulls the slobber covered muzzle out and allows the gun barrel to drop and naturally point to his heart. Even though his hand is still on the gun, he hasn't any strength left to hold it up. So, it slides down his chest and ends up in his lap. Again, pointed in a valuable direction. Not a muscle in his face has moved. His brain is numb and his spirit is dead too. He's acted this scene out many times over the years, but is still too frightened to kill the monster.

***

Danny walks into the drinking room, again. Someone is sitting at the bar, back facing Danny, as he moves to get a closer look from one side. It's a man, no older than he. Well-dressed, but somehow out of place, and time. Shiny slicked back hair, thin silk tie with a white dress shirt, and what looks like pleated gabardine pants with a really nice pair of leather shoes. As the man tips an amber bottle to take a drink, his cufflinks catch the light. *Old school.* Danny is still moving forward and thinks his guest appears to have stepped off the set of a 40's era gangster movie . . . matching the cars just outside his front door. He's inches away from the man and notices an onyx ring on well worked hands with a brilliant diamond mounted in the center of it. There's one just like it in his dad's old jewelry box, under his bed. The only things left to remind him he actually had a father, so he keeps them close.

There's something too familiar about this suave gentleman. Standing with a bottle at his side, he faces Danny. Nose to nose, same frame . . . same face . . . same blood. He commands Danny to close his eyes. Danny obeys like a small child. They're standing in a native cemetery where there are unmarked stones, weathered wooden crosses, and the ground is as solid as ice with weeds taking the place of grass – wildflowers are flourishing. The two men speak with their eyes. No words are needed to express the pain . . . separation . . . and disappointment. A mutual thing . . . only blood could understand. Danny closes his eyes and utters, "Daddy?" under his breath.

Back in the bar, his feet have been cemented in place. Breaking free, he races for the liquor cabinet, grabbing any bottle he can. Even Quervo begins to fly over his shoulders as he tosses bottle after bottle, the sound of breaking glass continues until each cabinet is bone dry and the smell of alcohol spilled all over the floor prevails.

"Evil spirit be gone!!!"

CHAPTER 11

The phone's ringing off the hook. Danny is unmoved, tangled in twisted sheets—pillows shoved off the bed onto the floor. His head is throbbing with the musty scent of his own sweat. Another rough night of doing battle with his sorted dreams. The phone continues to ring persistently longer than usual and the caller continues calling back and hanging up without leaving any message. *"I must be dreaming,"* looking over to see blurry green glow sticks, and lashing out at the clock with the back of his hand . . . *that's not where the noise is coming from? Not the clock!* Stretching even further to hear several vertebra crack, while reaching for the phone, he's unable to murmur a word. Just lying there listening to the intruder pervert the air. "We need you to speak again to defend our position!" Danny mumbles something in return that isn't close to being considered language and waits for a response. "Clean yourself up boy, you sound like hell!" Danny acknowledges the identity of the caller, "Chief?" The caller demands, "Be ready in a couple of hours!" Staring up at the ceiling, Danny's face remains pasted to the phone long after the Chief hangs up. The phone slips, bouncing off the hardwood slats.

***

James is making his way to a small private airport, where a corporate jet is waiting on the runway. Danny arrives shaven with a fresh tapered haircut and a business suit that's been hanging in plastic for over a year. Red power tie, a crisp white shirt, and a brand-new pair of leather shoes to replace the ones he ruined with the mud back in the forest. With leather attaché in hand, Danny climbs the steps to enter the executive's plane before the door is tightly sealed shut behind him.

Inside, six influential natives from other area tribes sit in the same business uniform, same blood red power tie. Danny draws several looks of concern from his peers. The tension in the air is stifling. Not one is engaged in any conversation. Taking the only empty seat up front, he places a set of headphones over his ears to break the silence, disengaging from the awkwardness of the moment.

Danny opens his eyes after coming out of a brief meditation. A mind dumping session of sorts. Not thinking about anything important. Looking around at the others in the cabin, he makes a judgmental statement to himself about their similar attire. *A white man's uniform of sorts. Ha!* He smirks at all the red power ties and recalls the history of it. Over two thousand years ago, a piece of cloth tied around a leper's neck to indicate they had the decease and a warning to others to keep their distance so as not to contract it. The idea that he's repeating history is rising to the top of his thoughts again. *What about the documents that all good native kids have read about?* Assimilated and having to discard ones culture in order to fit in.

The plight of a conquered people.

***

The jet lands and the steps extend to bite the tarmac. All seven natives descend from the little bird and swiftly file into their own limousines with several bodyguards at bay. *Purely window dressing.* Several even have chase cars with engines running.

It's been about forty-five minutes and they've almost reached their destination. The limousine dives head on into a sign carrying crowd, both pro and con native. The car abruptly stops directly in front of The Federal Building. The guard hops out from the passenger seat up front before the car completely comes to a stop and shields the compartment door like a G-man before popping the handle. *Another actor playing the part for a paycheck!*

Danny stands up, first out of the limousine, and gets grazed on the cheek with a tomato. A true red against his pale face. Not surprised at all, he continues to march forward hoping the others behind him will catch hell too. Pulling his handkerchief from his pocket, he gracefully wipes the ooze off of his stone face. All seven file up the cement steps to find a podium waiting without a microphone. Danny takes charge and places himself in the hot seat while he's being swarmed by reporters stuffing every major television station logo in his face, like he has something profound to say. A female reporter is the first to yell, "What do you think about the Government's charge to take back your land?" Another shouts, "Will you fight?" Danny thinks for a moment and counters with a question. "What would you do if someone came to your door and told you to get out?" A dead silence comes over the entire crowd. Then someone else shouts some ridiculous charge and the questions keep coming.

***

Danny holds his tongue throughout the entire return flight. The other six are finally talking, but arguing amongst themselves. After transferring into his own limousine, James suggests, "Pour yourself a drink, Boss." Danny proclaims, "I don't do that anymore!" James' eyes become wide with astonishment. Flabbergasted, his mouth open with absolutely nothing to say. *What in the world is going on?*

Up the cobblestone road, past the grand entrance, James drops Danny off around back. It's late . . . through his Eden, across golf grass to the greenhouse; he slips in through the back door. His suit jacket is draped over his arm, tie loosened, collar undone with tomato stains looking like blood from a hatchet attack.

Danny plops down on the sofa in the big-screen room like an anemic teen. He picks up the remote to have some sense of control over something and begins to serf. Stopping on his own image to watch his interview repeated on the late-night news. Pointing the clicker at eye level like a gun at his face on screen, he turns the power off in the middle of the question and answer session with reporters, walking away shaking his head . . . disgusted.

Time to hit the rack, totally exhausted.

CHAPTER 12

The morning sun gently finds Danny's face. He wakes without any nightmare to throw his slumber, not one ugly thought. This event, this energy, this peaceful rest is unknown. Confused, he heads straight for the bar without really thinking about it, robotic.

Danny struggles to remember that he swore off alcohol. He reaches into a drawer and pulls out instructions for the never used espresso machine. He pauses to think out loud, "Whatever ever happened to a simple coffeepot like my mother used to have, the kind that percolated?"

The phone rings. Danny picks up to hear Chief babbling vulgarities at the top of his lungs before he can get his ear anywhere near the receiver . . . this can't be a good sign. "What in holy hell did you do out there?" Danny sets the phone down on the countertop and continues to read on how to make an espresso. Chief is still beside himself and continues to curse wildly. Danny packs coffee grounds into a spoon like thing with a handle and hooks it up. He pushes a button on the machine and liquid begins to flow. Chief is down to a gurgle and it's not hard to figure out that he's enraged about what was said at the press conference, or maybe the way it was said. Danny is confident about his responses to the line of questioning the reporters delved out.

I was open and honest this time, speaking from the heart. Not anywhere near trying to be politically correct, not like before. When we were trying to secure the position of gaming on the reservation, everything we did had duality. Political with the public, half generous—half-cocked. Everyone could feel it. Even the politicians that rallied to our side knew that there would be other battles to fight in the future, and if we gave them enough money and a mission, then why not play political mercenaries for a handsome reward? They have families to feed too.

Watching the machine stream black crude into a ceramic mug, Danny bends to look deep into it. As it fills less than half of the mug, he complains in his head about the little amount that comes out, but not having any clue as to how strong it might be. The bubbles subside . . . he examines his reflection. Like a rock thrown into a lake, ripples blur his image and a large man emerges in his place with small wireframe glasses, dreadlocks like a buffalo. He's almost the same color as the coffee and begins to play the folk guitar he has clinched in his hands. The music is soothing and has something to do with a crow falling and eternal strength, I think. Danny pours a small amount of cream into the mug just to get rid of the vision. Disturbed, he picks up the Bat Phone at the bar to summon James. Oh yeah! Chief has gained a second wind and is still pronouncing his Chiefness on the other end of the line. James picks up and Danny commands, "Casino in ten!" Danny doesn't wait for a response before hanging up and James is already making a mad dash for the Bat Pole. What some people won't do for a paycheck.

CHAPTER 13

Danny steps into the casino. Like a cameraman, he pans the entire place and picks up a familiar feel for it. Noisy like a hen house, smoke-filled and already burning the back of his dry throat, he focuses in on his particular card table and takes a long look at the same players that were there when he left. The same two guys that were fighting before have become scheming buddies. Same mechanical look on the dealers face. Same pit boss wandering the floor waiting for some action. The only thing that's changed is the new victim that's taken Danny's seat, native too. Not another step, Danny turns around and leaves this hypnotic place behind. James is already down the road, believing that the boss will be consumed for at least the next three days. *Time to enjoy some sense of a real life!*

Danny could just call his driver back but welcomes the long walk home for some time alone. He throws his overcoat over his shoulder with one hand in his pants pocket fiddling with change. Cigarettes fall out onto the ground as he continues walking. Looking back for a split second but doesn't bother to pick them up. Cognitive memory charts his path, remembering what the reservation looked like when he used to walk home from school. "Grandma, you sure were right about all that would change. I don't think anyone could have imagined all the things that happened so fast. You probably didn't have much time to yourself as you helped all of us grow up. You saw us for who we would become . . . if anything. Who was I supposed to be?"

Danny makes it to the cobblestone and stands at the base of his hill looking up at his designer mansion, like a stranger coveting what he doesn't own. Today, his dwelling noticeably doesn't fit its surroundings . . . a mausoleum for the dead.

"This life has limits to achieve.
The eagle knows this.
It soars to its hearts content,
Living each day
As if it's last."

"As a child,
I danced and sang,
Perfectly in tune with nature.
Not missing a beat,
Or step."

"Now, I am awkward,
Out of breath,
Out of balance."

Danny marches up the hill with a conqueror's mentality!

Dizzy and breathing heavily, Danny is dying for a drink, but he's determined to stick to water on the rocks. Today, he could break through the front entrance, but keeps to his code and drags himself around back. He tugs on the little gate and sees that the spray misters are working overtime to keep Eden lush, especially out here in this desert. He stretches his neck overhead to place his mouth over one of the spigots for a minute of refreshment. Continuing through his forest, straight for the workshop, he darts across the clearing and enters a small room and pulls the chain on a single hanging light bulb above a workbench, turning to hang his overcoat on a pegboard hook behind him. After removing his shirt and placing it on another hook, he grabs several tools from the rack, as if he knows exactly what he's doing. Turns back around and pulls a plastic bag out of a metal drawer after having to hurdle yet another bottle of Especial. He pulls it out and sets it way out of reach on the end of the workbench. The bag in his hand contains a series of coyote bones that are relatively the same size. These childhood toys were used to play a native gambling game called Peon. Emptying the bag and spreading them on the bench in front of him, he pulls the stool out to take a seat in order to get down to business. He'll be here for a while. Danny reaches for his goggles and begins to drill and shape the artifacts.

***

Emerging from fine particles of bone dust, a traditional native breast plate has been constructed. His people weren't known for making war like other tribes across the plains, but he struggles with his feelings and senses a fight on the horizon. Danny moves quickly across the clearing into the greenhouse and temporarily places the protective vest on a table so he can gather several clay bowls from underneath it. He places the bowls on the table and reaches into a cabinet above his head. A grinding stone is found and he begins to crush several types of red berries. Each bowl has its own special concoction . . . a different hue. He cradles the paints with one arm and grabs the breastplate with the other hand while making his way back to the workshop.

Back on the stool, he props a mirror up to view his upper body. Using his palms like a brush, he pastes a deep blood red to one side of his face and an off white meal powder to the other. He dips his thumb into black gun powder and forms a line with it from the top of his forehead, down the bridge of his nose, over the tip, across his lips and stopping down under his chin. He takes two crow's feathers and does the best he can to twist them into his short defiled hair. Ashamed and guilty for the life he's been wasting, he takes a long look at the reflection of himself as a Brave. Something's missing. He takes a large military knife out of another drawer and pulls out his lighter to heat it up. Taking the blade to his forearm to drain some blood onto the counter. Dragging two fingers through it, he hits his cheek with them. Again, through his blood and then the other side. Even though his paint isn't close to being perfect, he really likes what he sees.

Native.

CHAPTER 14

Danny steps out of his workshop transformed. Not willing to enter the main house, he takes a new path towards the tree line, one he's avoided for too long. It opens up on the backside of his hill. There's a cliff overlooking a breathtaking valley of modernization. It must have been something to see back in the days before it was polluted. Stepping up on top of a boulder to look out past the city, all the way to the ocean, he admires the magnificence of creation. The sun is dancing on the horizon about to fall.

"A native stands boldly
Upon a megalith,
Overseeing what I have placed
Before him."

"Winged creatures pass overhead;
He wonders why he can't fly—yet.
Everything else has its place;
He's been given a much greater purpose."

"He was made as caretaker of my earth,
Not destroyer of it.
To blend with picturesque sceneries,
Not to devour them."

"My earth knows
His weight upon its surface.
He can remain mute,
And I will be aware of his every thought."

"I Am—The Creator!"

He steps away from his solid platform. The pine needles look to have woven an inviting place for a nap. Before night captures day, Danny collects some firewood. Reaching into a leather satchel, he pulls out the casinos brand of matches to light the kindling, "Sure is easier than rubbing two sticks together." He reaches in the bag again and selects a gourd, actually a rattle that belonged to his grandfather. He begins to warm into a steady rhythm and mimic what might have been his forgotten language.

CHAPTER 15

Next morning.

A field, lush with flowers. Danny, still in Brave attire, not poised for war . . . not a weapon in reach. Both of his hands are wrapped around a pine critter flute. The beauty of the notes flow from his memory of Grandfather dragging him to church every Sunday. You can hear the words resonate . . .

"Amazing Grace . . .

How sweet the sound.

Was blind, but now I see . . ."

***

A train of cars . . . six black, ominous government vehicles, stirring up havoc on a thin dirt road. At the edge of a field, he's marveling at the building dust devil twirling his way. Stepping from the wildflowers into the center of the road, he stands loosely with his feet apart; arms crossed low in front of him, flute still warm . . . hardly a smoking gun? The cars break off into a tactical position around the Brave, stopping long enough to allow the trailing cloud to pass. Federal agents step from their chariots, as if an ambush is ensuing. Danny finds humor in their behavior and cracks a large smile followed by a boisterous laugh. One agent approaches and meets Danny face to face where he stands. Black suit, black tie . . . a familiar friend from his childhood past. "Ya 'at 'eyy!" Danny responds by grasping the agents forearm and shaking firmly, like natives do.

He feels a prick on his arm and the clouds begin to spin in every direction before everything turns black.

CHAPTER 16

There's the sound of something moving around in the dark. A rat? No, definitely larger. Maybe something subhuman. Whatever it is, it's huddled in the corner of a small room rummaging for something. There isn't enough light to make out the creature.

***

Desperately attempting to start a fire, sweat pouring off his face, Danny's hands are on fire from friction and beginning to blister. "This is no easy trick!" A little smoke begins to rise after spinning a short two foot long dowel into a little thin block of wood for about four minutes of intense labor. Taking the block in one hand, he grabs some shredded paper with the other for kindling as he cups his hands and gently blows into them to ignite a fire. The smoldering ball is placed into a metal cup as the flame begins to rise. Danny lights a waiting candle and lifts it into a holder made out of several pieces of cigarette pack foil, placing it on a board just a few feet off the ground. Without wasting a moment, he goes straight to a thick book he pulls from his library and begins to read aloud, "At my first defense, no one came to my support, but everyone deserted me." Eyes wandering away from the page, they're filled with the reflection of the candle's flame. No hint of anger, or hatred to be seen in them. Things that would be expected of someone in his situation.

Someone is approaching from down a long tiled hallway. Peering through a small square whole in the door at eye level, a guard finds Danny balled up on the floor pretending to be asleep. The guard bends down in front of the door and picks up the usual ten letters a day headed for the outside world. Looking them over quickly, he pulls a small writing pad and pen out of his shirt pocket and jots down the names of the multiple states they're going to be sent to. His only concern is the daily betting line the guards have created to see which one can come up with the highest number of matching states closest to Danny's outgoing letters. The centurions can only wonder what a nut like this could possibly have to say to anyone. Or, if anyone would even care to listen. Every day, same thing, and all he gets in return is a couple per week.

After the sentinel completes his duty, Danny moves up off the floor to a board propped up between the toilet and a small metal trash can, a homemade desk. The letter he is about to write has been on his mind for weeks now and he's finally get it out. It's a hard one to even think about writing.

***

Cynthia,

We used to bump into one another in familiar places, sitting and talking for hours, as if there was some kind of psychic thing going on between us. I'd never tell you that you were always on my mind, but you seemed to know there was something more than friendship waiting. I loved how you kept your distance out of respect for yourself. Especially me being the way I was.

We grew up together, and I didn't know so many things about you until after the divorce. I didn't see how ridiculous I had become either. I also didn't quite understand the fact that you chose to love me because I didn't hunt you down like a wild animal. Although, I wanted to. Restraining myself out of an intense love for you was no easy task. Sounds so Romeo and Juliet. When the respect ended, so did the relationship. Why is it I always learn way too late?

The walls of this empty cell can't confine the many thoughts I have of you. We still take long walks in the forest and settled down over a fire on cold winter nights. I dream of the children, and how mischievous they might be because of the way we've been, like children playing. I know you're aware of what's happened to me. Although, the truth is no doubt jaded, I don't expect sympathy by giving you my version, but here it is anyway:

The family committed me here in order to get rid of me as the speaker of our tribe and potentially the entire Indian Nation. My influence among our people was growing. In the weeks that preceded the kidnapping by federal agents, I was beginning to generate a great deal of support from tribes across the country. Many of which opposed our position of what they saw as greedy selfish gain, and others weren't happy with the amount of funds we choose to distribute freely to less fortunate tribes without provocation. It never seemed to be enough no matter how we cut it up. It's unfortunate that I'm talking about our own people here.

Speaking honestly, not politically, in front of the Federal Building the last time was my undoing. It has landed me in this facility where I've been placed in isolation "for my own safety." Guess whose money is keeping me locked up? Freedom of speech is still a civil right and I crank out ten or more letters a day to many more tribesmen across the country. They don't allow me to have a computer. Most call me a political prisoner, and I'm sure you've seen the bumper sticker. I like the one Hero or Hostage? Someone sent it to me in the mail and I stuck it on the inside of my toilet seat lid just to have something to laugh about. I don't believe any sticker is going to move me closer to daylight for quite some time. Part of my rehab is to dispense with the notion of having been wronged and to simply stuff meds down my throat 'til my brains turn to mush. The nurse is supposed to check to see if I'm cheeking my pills. But, I gave her so much hell in the beginning that she just throws them through the hole in the door without talking to me. I, of course, grind them into the cement with my heel, making the floor a nice shade of chalky white.

After the mess I made of us, I suppose you think I'm Chief Knucklehead. Especially, after having heard of me sleeping out on the grass and masquerading around in Indian regalia. To tell you the truth, it felt good to create some semblance of being native. If they'd let me have my larger packages, this cell would look like a native hut, but since that's not the case, I just burden the guards with Bird Singing and Feather Dancing on a tri-hourly basis. It's the only exercise I get!

I suppose I've learned a few things while having a little time out to do nothing but order my thoughts, or go crazy. One of my most prevailing is that I've learned so much from nothingness, and absolutely nothing from having everything, except how to become numb and complacent, arrogant and stupid. Of course you know this, having been there to see me turn into the monster. . .

CHAPTER 17

After having had a long hard day on her feet, Cynthia is reading the letter in her small two bedroom apartment. Children are sleeping.

. . . *I now understand what you meant in the restaurant downtown, when I last saw you quite a few years ago. I was embarrassed at the sight of my ex-wife waiting on tables after all the money I had . . . we had. You were right, I traded my life for other things and you had to go on without me to grow on your own, away from me. You've always been a strong and independent woman. I admire you for that!*

As for all the finances, The Tribe has one more on-res share to divide with the others now that I'm out of the picture and the house is probably looking like a scribble pad from all the graffiti left behind by all the up-and-coming teens having nothing else to do except wait until they turn eighteen to become wealthy. In Great-Grandmother's day, before our birth, to live a life on the reservation would have looked like death from her perspective. Many ran, and never looked back. Many more became Mexican. Now with money and politics, if you don't conform to certain standards you get targeted for elimination. The difference between conforming to res life and living away from it is primarily a large grip of money. Maybe someone else is doomed to walk the hallways of what we called our house. I feel for the greedy fool who steps through its threshold and falls into that death trap. It makes no difference to me, I'm just as isolated here.

It makes me laugh to think how much we paid to have it built. Remember, when you pointed out how crazy it seemed that we were able to spend six million dollars on a house that would never have any true value. We'd never be able to sell it to anyone since it's on reservation lands. We could have willed it to the kids, but thank God that's not going to happen. Hopefully, they'll choose a life away from all of that. In fact, if I ever get a chance to sneak back onto the res I'll make one big smoke signal out of it!

The only reason I still get the off-res allotment is so The Tribe can claim they take care of their own. What a joke! Not funny! Anyway, I've taken a chunk of money that they didn't get their hands on and all the checks over the past years and have purchased land across the country. Specifically, anything that had been taken from natives. My way of seeking retribution for past wrongs against the "Ingines," so to speak. Maybe, I'll just turn it all back into one big camp ground. Anyway, we as a native nation seem to have developed our own little worlds apart from what we should be doing, which in the end will leave us divided and conquered all over again. This time, it's our choice whether we turn from it to create something wonderful, or complete the prediction of our own genocide.

How do we band together? Where do we start? This has become my life's work while imprisoned. Out of about fifty letters sent out per week, I get about three responses from those that agree with my vision of an America lead with its original inhabitants in positions of power. An honorable calling don't you think? Even greater is many non-natives have logged on to the website to pledge their support, so I've been told. But you should read the nasty letters I get from natives that don't want anyone trading off their financial position for some pie-in-the-sky idea, as one guy wrote last week. The death threats are humorous too, because if they saw my living conditions they would soon realize that death would be a relief. How many would go back to living like Great-Grandmother did? At least I have a sink and a toilet with running water.

Doing something worthy keeps my mind focused on the positive, instead of dwelling on my circumstance. For a time, my shrink allowed me a book per week for mental growth. I pushed for more and by the end of the year was up to one a day. When she decided I was overloading, I met with a chaplain and got him to give me every book he could on the history of world religions and ultimately burned him out when he realized he wasn't going to convert me to his particular brand of religiosity. I ended up seeking masters of other paradigms of spirituality and had them send material. My bookcase is completely stuffed. I've been like a sponge in here, trying to make some good use of time.

I have many regrets, and a lot of time for self-examination. Day in and day out, I search myself and even pray. Communicating with the Creator, unceasingly, and asking for Wisdom has been the key in moving forward, even contained in this cell. I've been hungry and I've been poor. I've been poor and had riches. I have learned to be content in whatever circumstance I'm in. Once I realized that I wasn't just talking to myself, and that answers to my prayers were being revealed, I began to widen my thinking to understand the expansive nature of my spirit. There isn't any box for that!

***

The guard interrupts, by slipping a meal tray through the rectangle slot at the base of the door.

Taking a break for a moment, Danny places his hand on top of his writing pad. The room has fixtures for florescent lighting on the ceiling but the tubes have been removed long ago. Danny uses unauthorized candlelight, a rebel. Recalling military service, he gets up and takes a few short steps toward the food to put it through a series of sensory tests, seeing if it's been spiced with anything foreign. This slop checks out, and for a second he stops to give thanks for all that he doesn't have to worry about. While standing, he wolfs down a small slice of liver and crams every last pea into his mouth with a plastic fork, in a hurry to return to his thoughts. Danny places the tray on the floor and scoots it back through the slot with his foot. He sits again, realizing the letter is becoming heavy and decides to cut it short. Reaching for a box of envelopes, he plucks a crisp one out and places the letter in it. Pulling an old address book from the shelf, he digs through it and finds Cynthia's last known address to write on the envelope. He places a stamp on it knowing the odds of ever seeing the letter again, or getting any response is slim to none, so he simply writes "Danny in chains" in place of a return address before tossing it on top of another ten letters to go out with the mail for the next day. The eleventh one will send the guards into a tizzy and tilt the odds in their little gambling world.

Danny begins a soft rhythmic chant and pounds the ground with his bare feet while the sound of native drum plays in his head. This is his way of worshiping the Creator.

CHAPTER 18

I'm not quite sure if it was all the dancing, or my persistently off key Bird Singing, but maybe the fact that it drove several of the guards from watchman to inmate made a difference. Whatever the case, I'm standing on the outside of this state nuthouse with a plastic shopping bag in hand. Nothing more than half the belongings I came in with and bright green foam infirmary slippers for shoes. When I arrived I couldn't read the entry sign at the gate because of all the drugs they pumped me with. Shackled to the floorboard of a barred transport van. The only thing I do recall is the guy in front of me proclaiming he was a serial killer and the one behind was as quiet as a mouse. Not a good sign. It turns out, the "serial killer" was a child molester that didn't want to be killed while locked up and the "quiet one" was the mass murderer.

I suppose most people, upon release, would try to create some semblance of life as they knew it, before incarceration. I shudder at the thought of reliving my past. This is a new beginning—a fresh start. The ability to create an entirely new existence and build my spirit simultaneously. Something I never knew before this *character building* experience.

Today, I am totally **assimilated** from all of my former bondages. The most positive use of a word I was taught to hate. I am free to develop my purpose, path, and meaning for my life. While locked up, I developed a burden for my native brothers and sisters. Now, I'm charged to figure out a way in which to better their lives. To encourage my people to become spiritual leaders capable of running a nation, not limited to an Indian Nation.

Maybe, I'll write a book about all that's happened to me! Go back to school and study something useful! Travel the world and get a larger perspective on the way people live! All things are possible to me today. My only limitations are those I place on myself. I feel like I'm eighteen all over again with the world at my fingertips. Supercharged and ready to experience the rest of what life has to offer.

***

Danny has gained a calming reassurance about himself these days. Long-suffering and self-control have been imputed upon him and Wisdom is available for the asking. These are tools he knew nothing about before he was incarcerated.

A passerby can't help but stare Danny up and down in his homeless state. Danny just cuts through the physical mess and greets the observer with the widest smile he can muster and a sincere "Hello friend!" The passerby scrambles for cover.

Danny's hair has grown out over the years. *Chief Crazy Hair* has taken time to braid it for this big occasion . . . his freedom. Recalling the memory of Joe the barber and his sheers, he laughs out loud and thinks of a phrase he picked up along the way, "You must lose your life to gain your life," and finally understands the meaning of it!

Confident, he turns his nose in the direction that smells most pleasing to him. Looking ahead only as far as he can see, he strolls up the street willing to take on any challenge.

CHAPTER 19

I walked along for some time before I found someone who wasn't frightened by my appearance. Funny, if I were in the big city nobody would have even noticed me. The owner of a small mechanics shop offered a day's work and I readily accepted it. He also gave me a pair of old dust covered shoes he hadn't worn in ages. At the end of the day he said he'd never seen anyone work so hard for so little. Eight hours, a meal, and twenty bucks later, he invited me back for tomorrow's grind. I thanked him for his kindness and continued on the path the Creator had laid out for me. I guess most would say I'm a drifter, but I prayed for a mission and receive answers daily. Drifters don't have purpose or direction, do they?

***

Three years later.

There wasn't a day I didn't wake up thankful for my every breath. I was taken care of and felt like the richest bum on the face of the earth. Food, and a place to lay my head was never an issue, and my safety depended entirely on God's graciousness.

I'd been riding trains for a while, enjoying the country several times over. I really hadn't given much thought as to where the path would end. I just trusted that the Creator of the Universe probably had a better handle on it than I did. Finally, I found myself standing in awe outside a gated compound topped with barbed wire. Since an unfortunate experience in my army days, I have never come upon anything that reminded me so much of the Berlin wall. Was this wall to protect the dwellers within, or to prevent escape? Reminds me of the nuthouse I'd come from. I took notice of the intercom and cameras and moved to the side when an extremely long limousine, much larger than any I had ever ridden in, pulled up. A bodyguard strapped with the butt of a gun sticking out from under his armpit confronted me as to why I was standing there. I looked around quickly and focused in on a theater like poster case that was located to one side of the gate. I told the guard that I had stopped to read the information. He ordered me to run along, so I honored his request not to cause any trouble. Once the limo was secure in the compound, I went back for a moment to officially read the information I used is an alibi. It was an advertisement for a native Pow Wow with a multicultural invite, taking place this weekend. I knew the area too well and headed for the festivities.

Most of us are driven to return home sooner or later.

CHAPTER 20

It's the peak of festivities and there's the wonderful aroma of Indian fry bread permeating the air. Danny is welcomed into a native dance by a large group of Feather Dancers in traditional costumes. Not one recognizes him as other than another native brother. He notices quite a few familiar faces, but they don't seem to remember who he was through their fog. *Probably ran out of peyote and smoked some sage to get by. Makes your head light.*

Outside the circle of Native Americans are people of all cultures in their traditional dress waiting to show off their own version of culture through song and dance. African, German, and a multitude that boggles the mind. All on the same patch of ground. *Never seen anything like it.*

Danny begins to pound out a familiar rhythm he's practiced daily. His vision fades to bleach white after hearing a loud crack and the native drum sounds more and more distant, until the sound of thunder replaces them.

Caught in a cloud. Four horsemen of the Apocalypse adorned in warrior dress, feathered shields and painted faces, greet him. "We've been awaiting your arrival!" They're wearing horns of the bison and multi-feathered headdresses. All are uniform, except for their different colored stallions. The pale horse is noticeably a bloody mess, but all are splattered.

***

Absorbed in an indescribable kind of radiating warmth. Warmer than any love you've ever felt. Can you feel it permeate your soul? A voice like the sound of a thousand golden trumpets resounds in every piece of our being. Can you feel the vibrancy in the tone . . . its perfect pitch? We're elevated way above the clouds. Are you with me?

"Grace is complete!" The words echo off the inside of my head and remain ringing in my ears. *Ping!* I am wholly aware that we are simply the creation and the Creator has driven us here for this moment. When did I become so enlightened?

Blinded for a split second by light so bright, but straining my eyes to make out the outline of a sphere coming into view. A beach ball? No, the earth off in the distance as it comes into focus, like pictures from an Apollo mission.

The globe responds to the sound of someone blowing outward with a long consistent wind, beginning softly and increasing steadily in its intensity. Something like a hurricane ensues.

A flashing light moves swiftly through a cloudy expanse. The sound of a great multitude is gathering. An army poised for battle, four multicolored horses upfront. All warriors are armed. Some with spears, others with Tomahawks . . . cloaked in bone breast plates and war paint. The leader raises a double edged sword high above his head. Upfront with a bugle in hand, I raise it to my lips waiting for a sign to drop the first note . . . salivating at the thought of having to call everyone to charge. *On my mark.* The leader lowers his sword, and points it towards the earth. I sound off with the first three notes of Taps *(Day is done…)* and the leader launches from his perch high above like an eagle swooping down on a kill. The entire regiment tucks in close behind him. The regiment looks like a comet with a blazing trail of light that's been hurled in the direction of the earth. Barely able to see through hail fire, we've crashed with full force into something solid. I sense a quake of catastrophic proportion. Rising flames moving across the earth's surface are devouring multitudes. The continuous shrill of bone chilling screams can be clearly heard! The sun is turning black like a smoldering coal in a fire pit and the moon is red, as if all living things have poured out their blood in one single instant. The stars are piercing the earth, torturing it like a pincushion. The planet quivers, like a piece of glass under pressure and explodes from the inside out into a centillion tiny shards.

I think to throw my hands over my face in an attempt to shield myself from harm, but can't find them. The entire universe is held captive to the brightest light you will ever experience, beyond nuclear.

Alive? How badly have I been mutilated? Frantic in my attempt to look around searching for my body, but not finding it. My flesh has been stripped away to reveal many truths. Purely conscience.

There's a surface as clear as crystal surrounding me as far as I can imagine. I've been enlightened to the fact that I'm the one on which the Creator chose to end all tangibly created things. The world as we knew it.

Resonating like the sound of rushing water, an audible voice proclaims:

"My New Creation!!!"

EPILOGUE

"Danny, get up! Let's get out of here!"

My wife's, ex-wife's familiar voice, coming through the heavy feeling that a ton of bricks had just been dropped on my head. The last thing I remember was feeling my knees hit the parade field. So woozy I'm gonna puke. Face first in the softness of the earth. Grass entwined with the hair in my nose. The taste of dirt on my tongue. A warm red fluid seeping down into what's left of my blurred vision.

I opened my eyes for a second and saw nothing but artificial light. I wonder if I'm still in heaven. Still in a place where no physical thing exists? A great place. I heard a female voice say, "Your wife is here and we're going to put a little something in your I.V." *Do I have a wife?* Then, I drifted off on Morphine high.

A few hours later.

"You really took a shot Danny! Nobody even knew you were in town until all eyes were on you after what your cousin did."

"And that was?"

"I can see how you wouldn't remember. He busted a large shaker over your head from behind and it sounded like thunder cracking over your thick skull."

"Huh, no doubt *[ridiculous chuckle]*."

"Blood spilled everywhere. I thought you were dead."

Remorsefully, Danny takes a moment to think. *It's all the same blood.* "There's a lot of that going around lately." *People killing people, brother against brother.*

Marveling at Cynthia for even being by his side, he considers it a great blessing to have someone stand by him in a critical moment. Mesmerized actually, like the first time he ever saw her as "a real woman." As children, they'd played out in the wash for years with all the other Indian kids. "Beat the Train" was best. We'd wait by the bridge for the smoke from the last of the coal powered freight trains to be seen from a distance coming from around the bend. Jumping on the tracks and navigating the railroad ties, just in time without falling thirty feet to our deaths before the train arrived. We'd stand on the other side and wave at the conductor with a mischievous look on our faces like, *"we beat you."* He was familiar with our game and never failed to smile and give a friendly wave.

Now that I think about it, he may have even slowed the train down knowing we would be hurrying to make the other side of the bridge. Cynthia was often out in front of the group without fear, she was a true leader even though she was the youngest. I always thought I'd be the one to fall, but knew she was always there to save me.

That little girl turned into the most desirable lady in my life. We got married in church, started a family, and did what people do with their time together.

Back at Cynthia's apartment.

I don't know how she did it, but she hustled my big butt off that field and into her little car and sped away to get me through the hospital emergency doors. No telling what would have happened if a whole mob had gotten a hold of me. I would have been stomped into the ground no doubt.

Twelve stitches in the pattern of a cross, and a broken jaw later, Cynthia offers a safe place to stay for recovery.

I had a lot of time to think . . . too much time really. But after having been locked up for years, I'd learned to sit still and wait a little bit longer for things to change around me. They always do.

The loud hard crack over the head must have sent me into a delirium while I was knocked out on the field. But was it just that, a delusion? It seemed as if time stopped. As if I really had been transported to another place, where time and space were of little use. The dream was all too real to be something of insignificance.

I spend the next several days playing the vision out in my head while Cynthia took care of me through the concussion phase. What I didn't understand was how I ended up with a wired jaw. Cynthia filled me in on the couple extra shots I got with a boot to the side of my face once I was on the ground. That's why she's been feeding me different kinds of clear soups through a straw and trying to make sure I'm comfortable.

Not having the ability to talk too well serves a purpose and keeps me out of trouble with her. She knows it hurts to smile, but when I'd do it anyway, because I'm acknowledging her kindness towards me, she warms over. I also have had a moment to sit back with my thoughts about how she could possibly care for me through everything I put her through over the years. It was me that became an island unto myself. She remained consistent. Something I still have to learn in this next stage of life.

Strange thing. I am somehow enjoying this moment. A moment in which she has taken time out in order to care. Reminds me of Grandmother. Someone who did it because that's just who she was.

Cynthia is a strong and beautiful woman, inside and out. Not to be qualified by expectation, but because she is everything the Creator has made her to be—a patient and loving future leader of her people.

GENOCIDE YELLOW: UNTIL DEATH DO US PART

A love story, and part two of a three part series. Danny Arrow has seen what life had to offer as a wealthy young native without purpose. Now, after years of trial and tribulation he has come to grips with himself and realizes he can't do much in way of great things as the individual he used to be. Cynthia, his ex-wife, is key to any success Danny will achieve, but coming to that realization is the most difficult part for such a strong willed person. You will see him struggle once again with himself, but not without his other half cheering him on and providing the foundation for growth.

A scary thing change is, especially when it can lead to success in the most challenging aspect of life itself— *LOVE*.

The X Chapter
Introduction

After digging through papers I'd stuffed away deep in the recesses of my closet, I discovered I hadn't picked these notes up in years. They were typed on paper that had turned yellow, three-hole punched, from the last typewriter I ever owned. Something my mother had given me. She's been dead for seven years this month.

I discounted the initial theme for the book as a story already played out on film and in books, history retold too many times. Not that it didn't have validity, but like so many true stories it gets lost in the annals of history and we are doomed to repeat its mistakes. I struggled for a bit and went another direction, a modern day story line. I'm including *The X Chapter* here for the curious, like myself. Those who enjoy "The Making Of…" type stories. Also, to note an accurate chronology of how *Genocide Red* came about. It isn't included in the front of the book because of its odd nature. I felt it would take away from the brevity of the story I ended up with. But it was the beginning of what started turning the wheels in my head on the writing issue. The most difficult challenge I've had to face.

THE X CHAPTER

(Original Title: The Gestapo)

I was a member of *The Gestapo* when I chose to exercise my right of religious freedom. Not according to the code I swore by, but in relation to basic human rights. You see, I had gained a moral obligation to another human being who was about to be misused for unspeakable purposes. My convictions were strong, and I had exercised these rights recently without being discovered. So I was confident I could go unnoticed, I was wrong. The duality of having to do a certain unconscionable job and having a conscience at the same time rose to the top. I became an anomaly among my peers, not hard to discern.

My interrogation began, as I was ordered to report to SS headquarters from the radio attached to the thick shiny black leather belt wrapped around my thirty inch waist. It held several tools of the trade to encourage compliance from unwilling rogues who didn't agree with The Gestapo's vays of doing business – a hand gun loaded with Talons, pepper gas, and restraints.

"SS-12 report, Mach Schnell!"

Another officer had been sent to take my place, so I dropped the metal boxes containing the *gold* I was tasked to load into metal cages and transport to the refinery, back of house, where the slave labor would diligently count the daily collection under the watchful eye of a camera. There would be a steady stream of victims waiting at the doors to fill the next set of containers with all that was left of their worldly possessions.

I moved my highly polished boots across the floor knowing that a trip to the commandant's office was only reserved for extreme circumstances and didn't usually warrant a pat on the back for a job well done. I had been there before and knew all I could do was act ignorant of my actions and not give away too much when asked about anything. *Just play it cool.* But my physical reaction to all of it was difficult to curb. Entering the office, my high-and-tight hair stood on end like any fine Bristol brush. The ominous dark uniform I was leased had picked up static and gave me a shock when I knocked on the metal door to request entry. Standing at attention, I waited for a reply.

"Enter!" in German.

I did, and didn't say a word. I scanned the small room about the size of an officer's quarters, which was stuffed with three of the most ranking SS on duty that day.

"Platz!" *(A dog command).*

No nonsense. I sat down and was ordered by the commandant to render secret documentation on an investigation I had been asked by the captain to conduct several weeks earlier. We we're on the verge of sending a few undesirables to the crematory with only a few more days to tie up some loose ends of investigation.

Unbeknownst to me, the commandant had been ill informed about the entire situation and was not happy at having to leave his elaborate office at command central to deal with this issue here at the prison. A dirty place . . . death looming on every breath.

I was placed under house arrest and escorted by a superior officer to my vehicle where the body of the investigation was secured in a locked attaché in the trunk. I retrieved it and was transported back to the office where an obviously irritated commandant was waiting impatiently. He had me open the brief and didn't really take any time to look at anything in it. Shuffling a few papers around, he pretended to show interest. *Not a good sign.*

With methodical coldness, he peered at me from behind his wire framed glasses and barked outlandish accusations to elicit a defensive response and provoke me to anger. I remained silent, which drove him to become flustered. As I said, this wasn't my first opportunity to see how *it* works. Special treatment. The lieutenant that had been attached to my every move grabbed the case and dug through it with demon like enthusiasm, as if looking for something specific. Meanwhile, another accusation was hurled from across the table.

"You have zex wit tha girl?"

I made the mistake of answering curtly.

"No."

On that, the commandant condemned me—*Guilty*.

The charge was severe, a violation of Nuremburg Laws, which state no outsider involvement. In fact, involvement with even your own kind off facility was an unwritten violation. The SS wanted full loyalty. Anything other than that was considered an overt act against the administration itself.

The lieutenant stopped digging for a moment to shoot me an empathetic glance, then went back at it with feverish pitch to discover a card of thanks that had been sent to me by a victim in the circumstance I was investigating. The reason it was in the brief to begin with was I saw it as part of the entire portfolio. Although, it would have been purged by me before presentation of the evidence knowing how involvement was viewed by command. See, the lieutenant knew well of the commandant's skirt chasing while visiting the facility. A common point of amusement among the troops. Even if I had been guilty of the accusation, she couldn't help note the contradiction of it all. Skirt chaser accusing another of the same.

The next words out of his mouth told me I was correct in my assumption that he had little to stand on.

"I'll give you a couple days to think about what you've done."

He had no real ground and would need a few days to trump up some charges and get the paperwork submitted to headquarters. In the meantime, I'd be left to flounder. Even have time to think about killing myself. That would solve everything for everyone, right?

After those final words of wisdom I was escorted off the compound by the lieutenant without my badge, and stripped of my dignity.

As we walked towards the exit, I turned to look over my shoulder while headed back to the lieutenant's vehicle. I recall thinking that this was probably my last look at the inside of the facility. *I got out alive!* Not in the way I would have liked, by my own volition, but at least alive. We stopped at the check point before exiting. I had nothing left to check at the door accept the awkward look I returned to my fellow troop as if the voice had been drained from both of us. But it was there. The knowledge of what had just happened. Another wrongful termination. Who's next?

Cameras were mounted on all four corners of the compound and I could hear the one closest to me spin in my direction. That was nothing. I had become used to the hundreds mounted in the interior of the ceiling that followed you around the entire day. Occasionally, when you'd get bored on the grave shift, you could do things in front of the camera to make the guys behind them laugh. Later, in the dining facility, they'd tell you how you made their day by lightening it up a bit.

We got in the vehicle in route to the parking lot a mile down the road. The lieutenant looked straight ahead the entire time without saying a word, like any good Nazi should. She watched as I got out next to my vehicle and actually had the audacity to wish me well. As if she knew I would never return. Can't really blame her, no one ever did return.

***

Astonishingly, I was called back several months later after the commandant and his crew were under many suspicions. I was returned to work by an authority above their level. Of course, stepping back into the environment was an acting job. Pretending that all that had occurred hadn't moved me a bit. Although, I was deeply hurt that I had been mistreated. One workmate gave me a nickname that stuck . . . Lazarus, because I had returned from the dead.

Within a month of my return, the entire upper level administration was completely relieved of duty. The commandant that had thrown accusation, the captain that remained silent over directing me to conduct an investigation, and the lieutenant that had watched it all go down knowing it was yet another misuse of authority.

***

Today things are different. Last week, an officer was written up for smoking at the back door at the conclusion of his lunch. The rules state, "No smoking in the public eye." Refusing to sign the document, he was slapped with an insubordination violation. He contested that fellow employees were not "the public." His superior wrote, *Sometimes supervisors make mistakes, however, insubordination will not be tolerated.*

We often make light of our situation by relating the work environment to a dog pound. *You never know who's gonna get it next.*

The Gestapo is still in fine form I zee.

ABOUT THE AUTHOR

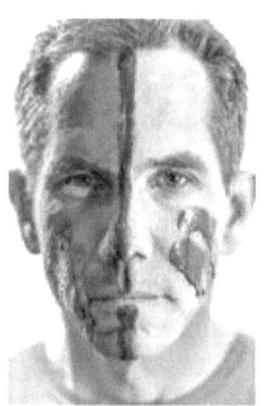

Dan Arrow is a novelist, publicist, and publisher looking to make a living from his efforts to discover and produce quality stories. Dan has been asked numerous times about his process of getting a book produced. He has become a book mechanic of sorts, but that's not all. No matter where an author is in their process, he will figure out a solution to meet their goals. He's even working with one Christian author that published a book with a company and wasn't happy with the results. We're fixing it now to be released as a self-published work of the highest quality. Edited right, formatted right...re-done right! Not just taking her money.

Dan is tenacious and neurotic about helping a client produce a product that stands toe to toe with anything on the shelf. (He recently helped a poet meet a 25 year life goal with just a few suggestions, and was blessed when presented with the final product). Then, he walks an author through the quagmire of marketing the work and branding a "name" for themselves. An absolute diamond in a box of rocks! Someone you have to meet if you're even thinking of writing a book.

Currently, he just released ***So...What About Love?*** And he's working on his next romance novel ***Love Guru Vigilante Style (Before Christmas 2013),*** is knee deep in the middle of blowing on the fire that is ***Unbreakable Love The Brian Warren Story (Amazon.com),*** and is in negotiations to work on a resource book for the unemployed. Crazy busy . . . just the way he likes it!

For more information visit www.heartfeltnovels.com

Also, "Friend" him on Facebook at the Heartfeltnovels and Unbreakable Love The Brian Warren Story fan pages to see what else he's up to.